Ronesa Aveela

Born From the Ashes

Illustrated by Nelinda

A "Baba Treasure Chest" story

Dedication

This book is dedicated to all those who keep the magic of fairy tales alive from generation to generation, adding their own spins and twists to stories.

www.mysticalemona.com

A steady, light tapping like a woodpecker drilling for bugs tugged at her senses.

"Kerana." Dimna's disembodied voice drifted toward her.

"No, Baba." She snuggled under the covers, closer to a black cat. "I was floating on the breeze. It was such a beautiful dream."

"Get out of bed and dressed." Her grandmother rattled the doorknob. "We have to leave before the sun rises."

She groaned and set her bare feet on the clay floor. Shivers rippled through her body. Kerana grabbed her cell phone from the nightstand. A reminder she'd left for herself flashed onto the screen: *Happy Twelfth Birthday. Maybe someone will like me this year.*

She hoped her mother would at least call since she couldn't be here.

Why couldn't she have let Kerana stay at home instead of dumping her here for the summer—in this tiny village away from everything? No, she was too busy with her big promotion to bother taking care of her daughter, and nobody else wanted to put up with a brooding child. Baba was the last resort, even though Kerana's mother didn't like her own mother.

After deleting the message, she shuffled to the door and flung it open, shoving the device close to her grandmother's face. "It's almost three a.m. Why do I have to get up in the middle of the night?"

Dimna skirted around her and stepped into the room, placing a folded white garment on the bureau. "Wear this dress."

She curled her upper lip. "I'd rather wear jeans and a T-shirt."

"It's tradition. Part of your initiation."

Kerana's heart fluttered. "Initiation into what? Mom says ..."

She studied her grandmother's outfit: a loose-fitting black dress flowed to her ankles, and a white headscarf covered her yellow, thinning hair. For a moment, she imagined flames licking a bubbling cauldron.

"You're not really a ... witch, are you?"

"Don't speak such nonsense. Your mother knows perfectly well that I'm a znahar, a healer. Get dressed so we can begin. We have a lot to do today." Dimna closed the door behind her when she left.

Kerana waited until her grandmother's slow, heavy steps faded down the hallway. She snatched the dress and hurled it onto the mattress. The black cat crawled from beneath the covers and sniffed the garment, pushing the fabric with her paw.

"Mira, stop that! Baba will be angry if you rip it." She nudged the cat away only to receive a look that said, *"You didn't treat it any better."*

She picked up the dress, rubbing her fingers on the silky softness, and brought it close to her nose. "Mmm, lavender."

After slipping it on, she examined herself in the mirror, admiring the colorful flowers and butterflies embroidered around the edge of the sleeves and V-neckline.

"Look at me." She sighed as she placed her hands against her flat chest. "A child's body in a woman's dress."

Mira's yellow eyes blinked. The cat yawned before jumping off the bed. Her tail flicking, she crouched and slunk toward the curtains, where she pounced on a spider spinning its web along the windowsill.

"You don't care either!" Kerana wiped away a tear. "I wish I had a friend to talk with, even a cat would be better than nothing."

"Kerana, hurry!" Dimna yelled.

She smoothed the crinkles from the dress as she stomped down the hallway.

Kerana tossed back her curly blond hair and thrust her hands on her hips. "I'm here. Now what?"

Dimna stopped kneading bread and sucked in her breath. "You look as wild and beautiful as a Samodiva." After wiping her floured hands on a cloth, she rose from the chair by the fireplace and hugged her granddaughter.

Kerana shrugged her off. "I'm freezing. Let me warm up a little." She rubbed her hands above the embers.

"It's summer. If you ate more, you wouldn't be so cold. What are you going to do here during the winter?"

She shrieked, "Mom's going to take me out of here before then!"

www.mysticalemona.com

Her grandmother turned away to arrange items on the hearth. "She's already kept you from me for too long. We have to do this before you reach puberty."

"Do what?" Kerana steeled her eyes on her grandmother.

Dimna pointed toward the hearth. "Kneel on the broom. It's time to perform the ritual."

"I'm not doing anything until you tell me what you're going to do."

With sparkling eyes, Dimna said, "You're going to be my successor, the next znahar."

She backed away, her eyes wide. "I won't be called a freaking witch. People at home already avoid me because they think I'm strange. They'll hate me even more if—"

"Shush, child." Her grandmother came closer and placed her hand on Kerana's shoulder, rubbing it with slow, gentle circles. "You'll have power to heal and more."

"Power? That's crazy." Kerana didn't want power. She wanted to be loved.

"It's not. You're special. The Samodivi told me."

"You mentioned them before. Who are they?"

"Kneel now. We have to hurry." Dimna again pointed to the hearth. "I'll tell you that story later."

"I don't—" Kerana stopped.

The glare on her grandmother's face scared her. She kneeled on the broom, its bristles digging into her knees.

Dimna placed a lid on the podnitza where bread dough was rising. Using an iron poker, she cleared a crevice in the middle of the ashes and placed the clay dish within it. She scooped ashes over the covered bread with an iron shovel. Her scowl relaxed when she glanced at Kerana's pale face.

"Child, don't fret. I'm not going to hurt you. I'll explain everything I do so you'll understand."

"O-okay," Kerana said without taking her eyes off her grandmother.

www.mysticalemona.com

Dimna placed the shovel on one side of the hearth and the poker on the other. "Iron tools have the power to chase away evil, especially after fire has sterilized them. Even the broom you're kneeling on is for purification because it sweeps away all unclean things."

"Why—" She shifted her knees on the broom. "Why are you doing this to me and not to Mom?"

"I failed with her when she was a child because it wasn't their wish. I won't fail with you, too."

"Their? The Samodivi?"

"Yes, now let me continue."

From a wicker basket to Kerana's right, Dimna removed three stalks of dry wheat. She plucked three grains from one stalk and placed them on Kerana's right knee, then picked three grains from another stalk, placing them on the girl's left knee. From the final stalk, she removed another three grains and tossed them into the fire.

"Wheat has been offered as a sacrifice to the gods since ancient times," Dimna said. "This will purify you so you become a vessel divine power can flow through."

Warmth crept through Kerana's body. She stared transfixed at the embers glowing in the fireplace.

Her grandmother moved behind her and grasped Kerana's shoulders. "Now repeat the incantation after me."

"Yes, Baba," Kerana replied.

With clear, slow words, Dimna spoke and Kerana echoed her response.

"From the first nymph Thrace, to me, to you,
Health from me, from God, and from the Holy Mother,
I vow to remain pure and holy, upholding the creed of the znahar,
Never intentionally harming, never for personal gain.
I will heal body, mind, and soul ..."

After a few lines, the words became a blur. Although she repeated them twice more, Kerana's mouth recited the chant, but her mind drifted away to the time of their ancestors, the Thracians. With each repetition, the world around her dissolved a little more until she was afloat above the embers, radiating their heat.

Dimna spoke from behind her. "Now make the sign of the cross three times."

"Like we do in church?"

"Yes, child, but this ritual precedes Christianity. To our ancestors, it symbolized fullness in life and a bountiful harvest. Now cross yourself."

When Kerana did, Dimna removed a clay flower from the basket and handed it to her. "Touch this to your forehead, then your heart, and finally your knees, then make the sign of the cross again."

Kerana did as instructed and extended the flower toward Dimna.

"No. Place it on your left side," Dimna said. She removed basil from the basket and stirred it in a bowl of water, all the while reciting a blessing:

"God provides everything for cures.
From me to you,
From you to others.
My hands will become your hands;
My mouth will become your mouth;
My heart will become your heart.
Forever together to bring a cure.
Your lifted hand will cure;
Your spoken word will cure;
Your gentle touch on stone will cure;
Your gentle touch on fire will cure;
Your gentle touch on water will cure.
Everything you do will bring life and health;
It will bring wellbeing to all mankind.
God and His mother will help you,

All that you do will cure.
From me to you,
From you to others.
My hands will become your hands;
My mouth will become your mouth;
My heart will become your heart.
Forever together to bring a cure.
Your lifted hand will cure;
All that you do will cure."

She sprinkled the basil water on Kerana and placed the bowl at Kerana's lips. "Drink. This will give you divine power."

After Kerana took a sip, Dimna turned the bowl a third of the way around. "Drink again."

Once more her grandmother moved the bowl, and Kerana drank. "This will guide your mouth to speak, your hands to do, and your heart to feel everything that brings health and life to others."

"How?" Kerana whispered.

"Understanding will come in time."

Dimna brushed ashes off the clay dish and removed it from the fire. As she lifted the cover, a tantalizing aroma from the golden-crusted bread wafted around Kerana.

"This is dobra dusha, kind soul," Dimna said as she broke off three pieces. "The first is the mediator that transfers power from me to you."

Her grandmother ate the piece, then handed a second one to Kerana. "Eat this."

The warm bread dissolved in her mouth, and her mind exploded with thoughts and visions. She felt alive and free.

Dimna placed the final piece of bread high in the chimney. When done, she sat in the chair next to Kerana. "We now share the power of healing. You will receive all my power when I die, and you will continue the family tradition. You may now rise, my heiress."

She got up and stood in front of her grandmother. Dimna tied a red thread around Kerana's right wrist and pinned a geranium onto her dress. "These will protect you when we go out to collect herbs."

K erana set her willow basket on the ground so she could yank a thorny vine from her sleeve. A full moon shone on the bushes and other undergrowth crowding the forest path. "Baba, where are we going? It feels like we've been walking for hours."

"Hush, child. The forest is full of eyes and ears. We're almost to my secret herb garden."

Scooting closer, Kerana whispered, "Why couldn't we wait until it was light out?"

"Today is Eniovden, Midsummer's Day. Herbs collected close to dawn have magical power."

Kerana twisted the red thread. "How will this and the flower protect me?"

"Red is the sun's strength. They'll protect you from the evil eye." Dimna stopped and looked among the trees. "And the Samodivi."

Kerana shuddered. "Are you going to tell me who they are now?"

"They're nymphs who protect the woods, fields, and waters." Dimna crossed herself as she continued walking. "I met them where my garden is now. They taught me everything I know about healing. My grandmother had dedicated me to them when I was an infant. When it was time for my own initiation, she brought me here. The Samodivi made me their sister and gave me the gift of healing."

"Then why do I need protection from them?"

"They don't accept all humans. Depending on their mood, they would just as soon capture you to join them as they would want to make you go insane with their seductive voices." Dimna stepped into a clearing. "Here we are. Let's hurry and collect herbs. We need seventy-seven and a half different kinds."

"Why that number? A half herb is rather strange."

"Each herb has a remedy to cure one of the seventy-seven known illnesses that exist. The half herb is for any unknown ailment." Dimna bent and broke off herbs, placing them in her basket. "We'll use some to make a giant wreath along with the other women in the village. Every Eniovden, young girls step through it in a special ceremony."

Kerana remained silent while they collected the herbs, wondering how bad a fit her mother would have when she discovered what her grandmother had done.

"Please fill this with water." Dimna handed Kerana a copper kettle engraved with the sun, moon, and stars. "Then put the herbs in it and leave it by the porch steps."

She lugged the heavy kettle outside and set it down.

"Move it away from the house a little more," Dimna instructed. "It needs to sit under the stars for the rest of the night so the herbs are even more powerful."

"I thought being a znahar would be more exciting than this," Kerana mumbled as she pulled the kettle toward an open space. "Here okay?"

"Yes, that's fine. Now come inside. I have something important to give you."

She leaned against the door after she closed it. "Why didn't you teach Mom all this?"

"Your mother wanted nothing to do with our traditions. Even at a young age, she had grand plans. She was going to leave this little village and change the world." Dimna wiped away a tear. "And she broke my heart doing it."

"And you think I'm different? I grew up in the city where people believe in modern medicine, not ... magical herbs."

"Yes, you are different. Not everyone can understand the healing power of herbs. A person has to have a gift before she can be a znahar. I tried to force it on my daughter, even though the Samodivi told me to wait a generation before passing on the knowledge."

www.mysticalemona.com

"Mom never told me why she kept me away from you. What was she afraid of? This inheritance? Or do you have other secrets you're not telling me?"

"Wait here. My gift will give you a clearer understanding."

Dimna removed a key from the pocket of her dress and unlocked a large, metal padlock from a door off the kitchen.

"Why do you keep that door locked?" she asked.

Dimna turned her head toward Kerana. "I have powerful herbs in here. They'd be dangerous to anyone not knowing how to use them."

"How ...?" Kerana began, but her grandmother had already closed the door behind her.

She pressed her ear against the door. Inside, papers rustled and glass clinked. Her grandmother's heavy steps got louder, so Kerana scurried to sit in a chair. Dimna carried a tattered book with a leather cover.

"Baba, you're so secretive. What is that?"

Dimna set the book in front of Kerana. Her fingers trembled as she placed her granddaughter's hands on the cover. A tingling sensation vibrated through Kerana.

"My dear child, I'm getting old. This is the book of knowledge. It lists the herbs and their incantations." Dimna sat next to Kerana. "You must promise me not to tell anyone the spells. They'll lose their power if you do."

Kerana caressed the book, longing to open it. "I promise. Are you sure you're not a witch? Mom says it's evil."

"Don't pay attention to her. Ignorant people use the word 'evil' for things they don't understand." Dimna sighed. "My purpose in life is to heal as many village people as I can, not only their physical problems, but also emotional and spiritual ones. When they want to bear children, they come to me. When they want prosperous crops, they come to me. When the waters dry up, they come to me. I keep bad spirits away from the village. Some people are afraid of me because of these things, but they respect me, knowing I'm here to help them."

"Thank you, Baba." She wrapped her arms around her grandmother. "You make me feel special."

"You are, my dear. You were born to be a znahar, to help people." Dimna stood. "I'm tired. I'm going to rest before the Eniovden festivities at the school. I'll begin teaching you afterwards. You should get some sleep, too. The sun will be up soon, and we still have a busy day ahead of us."

"I will, Baba. Is it okay for me to look through the book a little first?"

"Yes, but don't read it out loud until you can feel the herbs in your soul. Each one will speak to you what healing cure God gave it." Dimna stopped at her bedroom door. "If you touch the herbs and speak the words before you have this knowledge, their magic can harm or even kill you or the person you're trying to cure."

Kerana thumbed through the book's frayed, yellowed pages, with Mira curled next to her on the bed. Mindful of her grandmother's warning not to say the words out loud, she silently read penciled notes scribbled next to drawings of plants.

Herbs, like humans, have vitality. Merely plucking an herb does not release its energy. God endowed each plant with the ability to communicate. The color of its flowers, the shape of its roots and leaves, and the type of stem are used to determine its healing capacity. Yellow flowers heal jaundice. Plants with red leaves or roots are essential for blood-related diseases. The leaves of a purple iris can reduce the effects of bruises. Flowers shaped like butterflies can lessen the sting of insect bites. But the flower alone cannot cure without the proper words recited at the time of healing.

Kerana read remedies and spells for making love potions and preventing a person from falling asleep. She raised her eyebrows when she read the specifics of Angelical: *This herb is associated with the angels. Therefore, it's used to protect people from evil spells or demonic attacks.*

"Vervain!" She laughed when she read the next one. "I've heard of this from vampire shows. This says it enhances magical powers and prevents attacks against the mind. I guess that fits. It prevented the vamps from controlling humans. What do you think of that, Mira?" She stroked the cat's back.

Mira stretched, yawned, and purred.

"I'm getting tired, too." She yawned, but her eyes continued to ravage the pages, each one more fascinating than the last.

She flipped to the next page. "With Nostrum, you can break down a stone wall. I don't know why I'd want to do that. What else?" Kerana yawned again. "One more. Elecampane liquid lets you communicate with animals."

Kerana sat up, startling Mira. The cat hissed and jumped off the bed.

Once again, she read the passage. "It would be so cool to talk with animals. I wonder if Baba has any of this."

She slipped out of bed and tip-toed toward the herb room. The metal lock wasn't closed. Grinning, she opened the door slowly, but the hinges squeaked.

"Why aren't you sleeping, child?" Dimna said with a groggy voice from her bedroom.

"I'm thirsty and wanted a glass of water."

Kerana paused, listening until her grandmother's breathing became steady. She stepped inside the forbidden room.

Dawn was breaking, lighting the room. Fragrant, dry herbs hung in bouquets along the back wall. A glint on the table caught her attention, and she checked it out. A golden cross was submerged in a flat copper bowl filled with water. Not what she wanted. What else was in the room?

A bookcase held multi-colored glass jars. "What's in this?" She peered at a shriveled snake head and shivered. "Gross. And that one looks like a bat. Where are the herbs?"

She squatted and read labels from the jars on the lower shelf. Geum, White Oman, Nostrum, Elecampane.

www.mysticalemona.com

Kerana's heart pounded. "That's it!"

With a trembling hand, she opened the purple bottle and sniffed. No smell.

She took a small sip and smacked her lips at its slight sweetness. "Maybe a little more."

"Kerana, finish your drink and go to bed," her grandmother's muffled voice said. "You'll be overtired for the celebration later."

Startled, Kerana almost dropped the jar. "Don't get up! I'm going now. Good night."

She quickly screwed on the cover and replaced the bottle on the shelf. After closing the door, she hurried to her room and picked up the cat from her bed.

"Mira, talk to me."

The cat opened her eyes and yawned.

Kerana frowned. "I'm so stupid to believe in this magic stuff. It's nonsense. Herbs can't let you talk with animals."

She crawled into bed and buried herself under the cold blankets.

Kerana woke to a rough tongue licking her face and sharp pin-pricks on her shoulder. Whiskers tickled her nose, and she sneezed. She opened her eyes to find Mira staring at her through yellow glass slits.

"Get up, dormouse. I'm hungry."

Kerana jumped out of bed. "Who spoke? Nobody's in the room."

"Well, I'm here." Mira swished her tail.

"I must be dreaming, or ... the herb worked!" Kerana snatched the cat from the bed. "Mira, say something else. Please tell me something."

"Let me go, Kerana. I'm hungry, and you've overslept."

"Yes, the herb worked!" She jumped around the room, then stopped. "I can't tell Baba. She'd be angry I used the herbs before she taught me."

She went into the kitchen, fed Mira, and kissed her grandmother.

"Happy birthday, dear," Dimna said. "With all the excitement this morning, I forgot to wish you health and blessings, and may all your wishes come true."

"Thanks. Today one did come true." Kerana smiled.

She had a friend to talk with.

After breakfast, Dimna and Kerana removed half the herbs from the kettle and wove them into a long strand.

"I'll dry the rest for my medicines." Dimna patted her wet hands on a towel. "Take this one to the school."

Kerana dropped the herbs. "You're not going with me? I don't know anyone there."

www.mysticalemona.com

"I'll be there later, but I have things to do here first."

"We can go together."

"No, the women need these herbs for their wreath." Dimna placed it into Kerana's hands. "There are plenty of girls your age you can talk with. They'll all be going through the ceremony."

Her shoulders slumped. "Another ceremony? Are they ... becoming znahars? I thought you said it was special, that I was special."

Dimna hugged her. "You are. This is a different ceremony to ensure our young women are protected from the zmey."

Kerana opened her mouth to ask what a zmey was, but her grandmother continued, "He's a dragon who likes to kidnap young girls when they're dancing. Not to be mean, of course. He has a tender heart and often falls in love with human maidens, and wants to marry them."

Kerana laughed. "Surely that can't be true."

Dimna curled her lips into a knowing smile. "Tell you what. Let me give you a quick znahar lesson. Grab a bowl and spoon, and join me outside."

It had lightly rained during the time Kerana had slept. Puddles formed pools around the driveway.

Dimna kneeled near one, and she motioned Kerana over. "The morning of Eniovden, I always gather dew or rainwater. It acquires healing power after the sun bathes in it. I use this water to make potions."

"Can we make something after the ceremony?" Kerana scooped water into the bowl.

"Yes, perhaps a cure for insecurity," Dimna said, her eyes filled with sadness.

earing the white, embroidered dress, Kerana yelled from the door, "I'm leaving. If Mom calls, tell her I miss her and love her."

She grabbed the twisted herbs and dragged her feet toward the school. Laughing and shouting filled the playground.

www.mysticalemona.com

She squeezed the herbs close to her chest and took a deep breath. "I can do this."

A dark-haired girl, wearing a dress similar to Kerana's, ran toward her. "Hi, I'm Sophia."

"I'm Kerana. My grandmother's—"

"The znahar. Everyone knows her." Sophia took Kerana's hand. "Come with me. We've been waiting for her herbs. They have special protection powers."

"Do you really believe a dragon will steal you to make you his bride?" she asked.

Sophia shivered. "I don't want to find out. Did you know the zmey's bride eventually grows a tail like his? One girl tried to bite hers off when she wanted to visit her family. She thought they'd be afraid, or even ashamed of her for running off and marrying a dragon."

"Were they?"

Sophia sighed. "She never made it home. When she heard her former friends singing down the road, the poor girl was in a frenzy to remove the tail before they saw her. She tore away at it so fast that her heart burst, and she died. It never ends well falling in love with a dragon."

"At least she had friends once," Kerana mumbled.

"You'll make lots of friends here." Sophia squeezed her hand. "I can already tell you're going to be my best friend."

The large room where women and girls twisted herbs onto a wreath smelled heavenly.

Kerana opened her eyes wide. "Wow, that's huge!"

Sophia laughed. "It has to be so we can walk through it."

"How do you add the herbs to it?"

"Like this." Sophia showed her.

Kerana picked up a bunch of twisted herbs and looked for a place to join in. The women and girls busily chatted away as they went about their task. Kerana hesitated and set the herbs down. "Sophia, I'm going outside to wait for Baba. Come sit with me when you're done."

"Don't you want to help?"

Kerana shrugged. "I don't want to miss Baba when she gets here."

Sophia hugged her. "Okay, I'll be there shortly. I'm not letting you get out of stepping through the wreath. I'd hate for a zmey to steal you from me."

K erana sat at a picnic bench under a gnarled oak. Children swarmed like bees around the playground, some waving to her. A flock of birds on top of the old school roof distracted her as they squawked and flew off in a rush. A couple of ravens landed on a branch above her and ruffled their feathers.

"I told you it was dangerous to land on the roof. Why don't you ever listen to me? Someone's been pecking at that wire and now it's exposed. Didn't you notice the sparks? It almost burned my feet."

"Yah, well my wing got burned, too. The flames licked my beautiful feathers."

Kerana jerked her head toward the birds. "What flames? What do you mean?"

The two birds looked down. The larger one said, "Who are you?"

"I know. I know." The other bird hopped on the branch. "She's the gifted one, Dimna's granddaughter."

"What about the flames?" Kerana asked. "Where are they?"

"On the school roof. Sparks from an exposed wire have ignited the roof," the smaller bird said.

In exasperation, Kerana yelled, "You said that already, but what part of the roof?"

"Hey, who are you talking to?" A boy riding a bicycle circled the tree. "Oh, you're the witch's granddaughter. Is she hiding in the tree with her broomstick?"

"Leave me alone." She glared at the heavyset boy, and took a deep breath, inching her way around him. "Real witches don't fly on brooms. They pickle heads of mean boys."

"Yah, and then you eat them. Either that or you fly around the forest to collect bats for dinner," the boy jeered. "You're a witch like your grandmother. I saw you both flying on brooms last night."

"Get lost, stupid boy. I have to go," Kerana said as she rushed off. "There's a fire in the school."

"What? Who told you that? I didn't see a fire."

"The ra— I just know there's one." The boy would think she was crazy, or maybe even decide she was a witch if knew she could talk with animals.

"Fire! Fire!" Kerana screamed as she neared the school. "Get everyone out!"

Several people rushed outside, but a woman standing by the door grabbed Kerana's shoulder, pulling her aside. "What are you talking about? There's no fire."

"The roof's on fire! Please believe me. I-I saw smoke up there. You have to get everyone outside now."

"She's crazy like her old witch grandmother, Mrs. Dimova." The boy laughed as he swaggered over. "She was jabbering away to nobody a moment ago."

Kerana started crying. "Please tell everyone they have to leave the building."

The fire alarm sounded, wiping the smug grin from the boy's face.

A thunderous crack came from over the cafeteria, and the roof collapsed. Glass shattered as the walls crumpled. Flames lurched from the gaps, hissing like a seven-headed dragon.

Mrs. Dimova pulled Kerana and the boy outside well away from the building, then dialed the fire department. "Everyone stay calm. The firefighters are on their way. Check to see if anyone you were with is missing."

Kerana looked for Sophia amid the frantic people shouting and screaming in the schoolyard.

A white mouse brushed against Kerana's trembling leg. "So much smoke. Your friend screaming. Door locked. Trapped."

She kneeled by the shaking creature. "Sophia? Where?"

"In the biology lab."

She sprinted toward the building.

A man grabbed her arm as she ran past. "Where are you going? The building's going to collapse at any moment."

"Let me go or she'll die." She kicked him in the shin, and he yelped, releasing his grasp.

People were still swarming out of the building. Children screamed for their parents. People pushed against each other as everyone scrambled past her toward the exit like frightened sheep.

"Where's the lab?" Kerana asked one person.

He pointed down a long hallway.

The intense heat bit at Kerana's skin. She groaned, inching a beam away from the door. A sea of smoke poured out, stinging her eyes. She coughed. "I'm here, Sophia. Where are you?"

Crying came from the wall next to her. She reached over and felt a body. Sophia's ash-smudged face peered at her.

"Thank God, you're safe." Kerana grabbed her hands. "Hurry now. Let's get out of here."

They were almost at the door when a beam cracked above them. Kerana pushed Sophia forward. "Go!"

A flame burst between them, blocking Kerana from the door. Sophia froze.

"Go! Now! I'll find another way out."

Another beam cracked and flames licked the air. Sophia screamed, "I'll get help," and raced out the door.

Smoke choked Kerana, and she collapsed.

"I love you, Mom. I love you, Baba."

Scorching heat and blinding light surrounded Kerana before darkness overtook her.

Firefighters raked through ashes and burning embers, all that remained of the school, looking for a body. One picked up a burned cell phone by the place where the front door of the school used to be. He handed it to the chief.

"I'm so sorry for your loss, ma'am. We couldn't find Kerana's body. She was brave and saved another girl, but lost her own."

"Oh Lord, my child." Dimna trembled, tears running down her face.

Mrs. Dimova wrapped her arm around Dimna. "No one believed her about the fire. How could she have known?"

"My Kerana was special. Where are you, my sweet child?"

"I'm here, Baba, trapped under a beam. Please help me." She struggled to make her way to the surface. Ash toppled to the side as she poked her head out. "Fresh air at last."

She waved to the people standing a few feet in front of her. Her grandmother continued to weep.

"Can't you see me, Baba? I'm right here."

Kerana beat against the ashes that encased her like a cocoon. "I'm so weak. Got. To. Try. Harder."

She wiggled around more until she was delivered from her ashen tomb. "I'm free."

"Look. What's that moving in the ash?" Mrs. Dimova asked.

A beautiful butterfly with red-and-black-striped wings like a burning flame rose from the ash. It perched on Dimna's arm for a moment, then spread its wings and fluttered on the breeze.

"I love you, Baba. Tell Mom I love her, too." She was free to soar higher than she'd ever thought.

***

In honor of Kerana and her heroism, villagers planted a colorful herb garden in front of the new school. Every summer a red-and-black butterfly with flaming wings returns to the place where her freedom began.

www.mysticalemona.com

www.mysticalemona.com

www.mysticalemona.com

33

www.mysticalemona.com

www.mysticalemona.com

www.mysticalemona.com

Acknowledgments

As always, many thanks to our critiquers, who point out all the ways to make our story better. Alexander, Aliya, Erin, and Jordan.

A special thanks to Georgi Mishev, author of *Thracian Magic: Past and Present*, from which we have based the znahar initiation ceremony. He has also graciously given us permission to use an English translation of the Bulgarian incantation found in the above book (footnote 113, page 85).

About the Authors

Ronesa Aveela is a collaborative effort by Anelia Samovila and Rebecca Carter. Please visit our website at www.mysticalemona.com.

Anelia is a freelance artist and writer who lives near Boston, MA. She likes writing mystery romance inspired by legends and tales. In her free time she paints. Her artistic interests include the female figure, Greek and Thracian mythology, folklore tales, and the natural world interpreted through her eyes. Anelia is married and has two children, a dog, and a cat.

Rebecca is a writer who lives in southern NH. She is an avid reader who has traveled around the world seeking adventure and knowledge of other cultures. Linguistics has inspired her since her initial study of Latin. But, mostly, she is known for her baking ability.

Our books:

Mystical Emona: Soul's Journey
Light Love Rituals: Bulgarian Myths, Legends, and Folklore
The Christmas Thief (A "Baba Treasure Chest" story)
The Miracle Stork (A "Baba Treasure Chest" story)
Born From the Ashes (A "Baba Treasure Chest" story)

Coming soon:
Dragon Village (A "Balkan Tales" story)

Reviews

PLEASE HELP INDIE AUTHORS AND LEAVE A REVIEW

We hope you've enjoyed this book. As indie authors, we would appreciate your review. Good or bad, we'd love to hear your honest thoughts.

Printed in Great Britain
by Amazon

82048331R00027